Cutting in Line Isn't Fair!

by Anastasia Suen
illustrated by Jeff Ebbeler

Content Consultant:
Vicki F. Panaccione, Ph.D.
Licensed Child Psychologist
Founder, Better Parenting Institute

Published by Magic Wagon, a division of the ABDO Publishing Group, 8000 West 78th Street, Edina, Minnesota, 55439. Copyright © 2008 by Abdo Consulting Group, Inc. International copyrights reserved in all countries. All rights reserved. No part of this book may be reproduced in any form without written permission from the publisher. Looking Glass Library™ is a trademark and logo of Magic Wagon.

Printed in the United States.

Text by Anastasia Suen
Illustrations by Jeff Ebbeler
Edited by Patricia Stockland
Interior layout and design by Becky Daum
Cover design by Becky Daum

Library of Congress Cataloging-in-Publication Data

Suen, Anastasia.
  Cutting in line isn't fair! / Anastasia Suen ; illustrated by Jeffery Ebbeler.
      p. cm. — (Main Street school)
  Summary: A group of children learns the importance of being fair and waiting to take one's turn.
  ISBN 978-1-60270-029-1
  [1. Fairness—Fiction. 2. Behavior—Fiction.] I. Ebbeler, Jeffrey, ill. II. Title.
  PZ7.S94343Cut 2007
  [E]—dc22
                                    2007004761

Latasha patted her hair as she walked to the front of the bus stop line.

"Is she trying to take cuts?" asked Jessie.
"You know Latasha," said Rachel.

Jessie and Rachel watched as Latasha talked to a girl in the front of the line. The girl shook her head.

"I knew it," said Jessie. "She's trying to cut in the line."

"Latasha doesn't like to wait," said Rachel.

"I don't like to wait either," replied Jessie.

"Here comes the bus!" said Rachel.

Jessie picked up her backpack.

"Look at that," said Jessie.
"Latasha is in front of us in the line!"

"What?" asked Rachel as she
turned around.

"They gave her cuts!" said Jessie.
"That's not fair!"

"She's with Megan," said Rachel.

"She still cut in line," said Jessie.

The kids climbed into the bus one by one.

"I'll look for a window seat," said Jessie.
"Then we can sit together."

"Okay," said Rachel.

But all of the window seats were taken.
Rachel followed Jessie to the back of
the bus.

The bus was so full they had to sit in
separate rows.

The bus driver closed the door and drove to the next stop. Jessie sat next to a boy she didn't know.

I wish I could sit with Rachel, thought Jessie.

Jessie looked at the front of the bus. Latasha was sitting by a window!

She cut in line and got to sit by a window, thought Jessie. *No fair!*

Miss K took attendance for the day. This morning, the third grade was going to the library.

Jessie and Rachel lined up when Miss K called their row.

"I want to read the next Mystery Girls book," said Jessie.

"I want to read the one you have now," said Rachel.

"Let's ask the librarian to check the book out in your name," said Jessie.

Then Latasha walked by.

"Not again," said Jessie. "Look, she walked right up to the front of the line."

"She's talking to Megan," said Rachel.

"Look, Megan gave her cuts," said Jessie. "Again!"

"Latasha and Megan are friends," said Rachel.

"I know that," said Jessie. "But taking cuts isn't fair."

Miss K's class walked down the hall to the library.

"Put your books in the book drop," said the librarian. "Take a shelf marker."

Jessie walked up to the librarian. "Can my friend Rachel check out my old book?"

"Of course," said the librarian. "Let me check the book in."

She put the book under the scanner. *Beep!*

"Now Rachel can check it out," said
the librarian.

"Thank you," said Jessie.

"Thank you," said Rachel.

"Let's get the new Mystery Girls book,"
said Jessie.

Jessie and Rachel walked over to the
shelves. But the book wasn't there.

"Where did it go?" asked Jessie.

Rachel looked around the library. "Latasha has it."

"Latasha!" said Jessie. "She took cuts and now she has my book! That's not fair!"

"What are you going to do?" asked Rachel.

"I'm going to ask her for my book," said Jessie.

Jessie walked up to Latasha.
"May I have that book, please?"

"What?" asked Latasha.

"You cut in line and took the book I wanted,"
said Jessie.

"I did not," said Latasha.

"Yes, you did," said Jessie.

"The book was just sitting there on the
shelf," said Latasha. "You weren't there."

"I wasn't there because you took cuts," said Jessie. "Twice!"

"Twice?" asked Latasha.

"You took cuts at the bus stop, too," said Jessie.

"We weren't at school yet," said Latasha.

"It's still not fair," said Jessie. "You took cuts at the bus stop and took the last window seat."

"It's just a seat," said Latasha. "It didn't matter."

"If it didn't matter, then why did you take cuts?" said Jessie.

"Why not?" said Latasha.

"The other people were there before you," said Jessie.

"Megan saved my place," said Latasha. "Doesn't Rachel do that for you?"

Jessie looked at Rachel. Rachel shrugged. "Sometimes," said Jessie.

"So you take cuts, too," said Latasha.

"Well," said Jessie, "I guess I do."

"I don't like to wait," said Latasha.

"Nobody does," said Jessie. "But that doesn't make it right to cut."

Latasha gave Jessie a look.

"Even when I do it," said Jessie.

Latasha looked at the book. "Here," she said. "I can read it next week."

"Thanks," said Jessie. "I'll save it for you."

Latasha smiled at Jessie and said, "Good. Then I won't have to cut in line!"

The girls all laughed.

What Do You Think?

1. Was it fair when Latasha took cuts at the bus stop?

2. Was it fair when Latasha found the new Mystery Girls book first?

3. Was it fair when Jessie took cuts from Rachel?

4. What would you do if someone took cuts in front of you?

5. Do you let your friends take cuts?

Words to Know

fair—reasonable and just.
help—to assist.
rule—official instruction that tells you what you must or must not do.
share—to divide something between two or more people.
trade—to exchange one thing for another.

Miss K's Classroom Rules

1. Take turns.
2. Listen to others.
3. Follow the rules.
4. Share.

Web Sites

To learn more about fairness, visit ABDO Publishing Company on the World Wide Web at **www.abdopublishing.com**. Web sites about fairness are featured on our Book Links page. These links are routinely monitored and updated to provide the most current information available.